THE BIG BOOK OF PAW PATROL

By
Mary Tillworth

A GOLDEN BOOK • NEW YORK

randomhousekids.com
ISBN 978-0-553-51276-2
T#: 314885
Printed in the United States of America
10 9 8 7 6 5 4 3 2 1

When Ryder calls, the PAW Patrol reports to the Lookout to get their rescue mission. No job is too big, and no pup is too small!

dangerous roads, or control a crowd.

Chase can also solve any mystery with his super-sniffing nose. But that mystery had better not involve cats or feathers, because they make him sneeze!

Chase's Pup House transforms into a police truck. In his Pup Pack are a megaphone, a searchlight, a net, and other things to help this police pup keep the peace.

MARSHALL

"I'm all fired up!"

Marshall is the PAW Patrol's fire dog. He's a Dalmatian who's always ready to race to the rescue—though his excitement often makes him a little clumsy. When running into the Lookout for a mission, he'll trip over his own feet, and even knock over the other pups!

But no matter what happens, Marshall always lets his friends know that he's okay!

Marshall's Pup House turns into a fire truck.
His Pup Pack holds a double-spray fire hose that
helps him extinguish all kinds of trouble.

skateboarding and snowboarding. He also has a soft spot for "itty-bitty" kitties and other cute critters.

Rubble's Pup House turns into a digger with a
bucket shovel and a drill. His Pup Pack opens into a
bucket arm scoop so he can dig into any situation.

SKYE

"This pup's gotta fly!"

Skye is the PAW Patrol's fearless, flying daredevil. This cockapoo pup may be the smallest on the team, but she's also the fastest, and she's always ready to fly off on any adventure!

Skye stays active by snowboarding and dancing along to her Pup-Pup Boogie video game, but she also takes time to get relaxing *paw*-dicures.

Skye's Pup House transforms into a helicopter.
Her Pup Pack has wings that pop out to help her
fly into action.

can often turn someone else's trash into his treasure. His motto is "Don't lose it— reuse it!"

Rocky can get a little scruffy because he's not a fan of baths. In fact, he doesn't ever like to get wet!

Rocky's Pup House transforms into a recycling truck. His Pup Pack includes many different tools and an awesome mechanical claw.

ZUMA

"Ready to dive in!"

Zuma is the team's water-rescue dog, a fun-loving Labrador and the youngest member of the PAW Patrol team. He's happy and energetic, and is always trying to get the more serious pups to lighten up.

Zuma loves the beach and anything water-related. This playful pup surfs, dives, and even enjoys bath time!

Zuma's Pup House turns into a hovercraft.
His Pup Pack holds air tanks and propellers
to help him dive deep underwater.

RYDER

Ryder is a ten-year-old boy who runs the Lookout and leads the PAW Patrol. He adopted and trained each of the puppies to be a part of one terrific team.

When someone needs help, Ryder calls the pups, picks the right ones for the job, and rolls out with them! And when the work is done, he makes sure they all get a well-deserved pup treat.

THE LOOKOUT

The Lookout is home and headquarters to the PAW Patrol. When Ryder gets a distress call, he calls the pups, who gear up during the elevator ride, get their mission at the top floor, and then slide down into their Pup Houses, which transform into vehicles. Then they roll out to save the day!

At the top of the Lookout, the PAW Patrol watches over the whole city and responds to any calls for help. The pups gather for their mission here, and Ryder organizes the pack and decides which pup is best for the job.

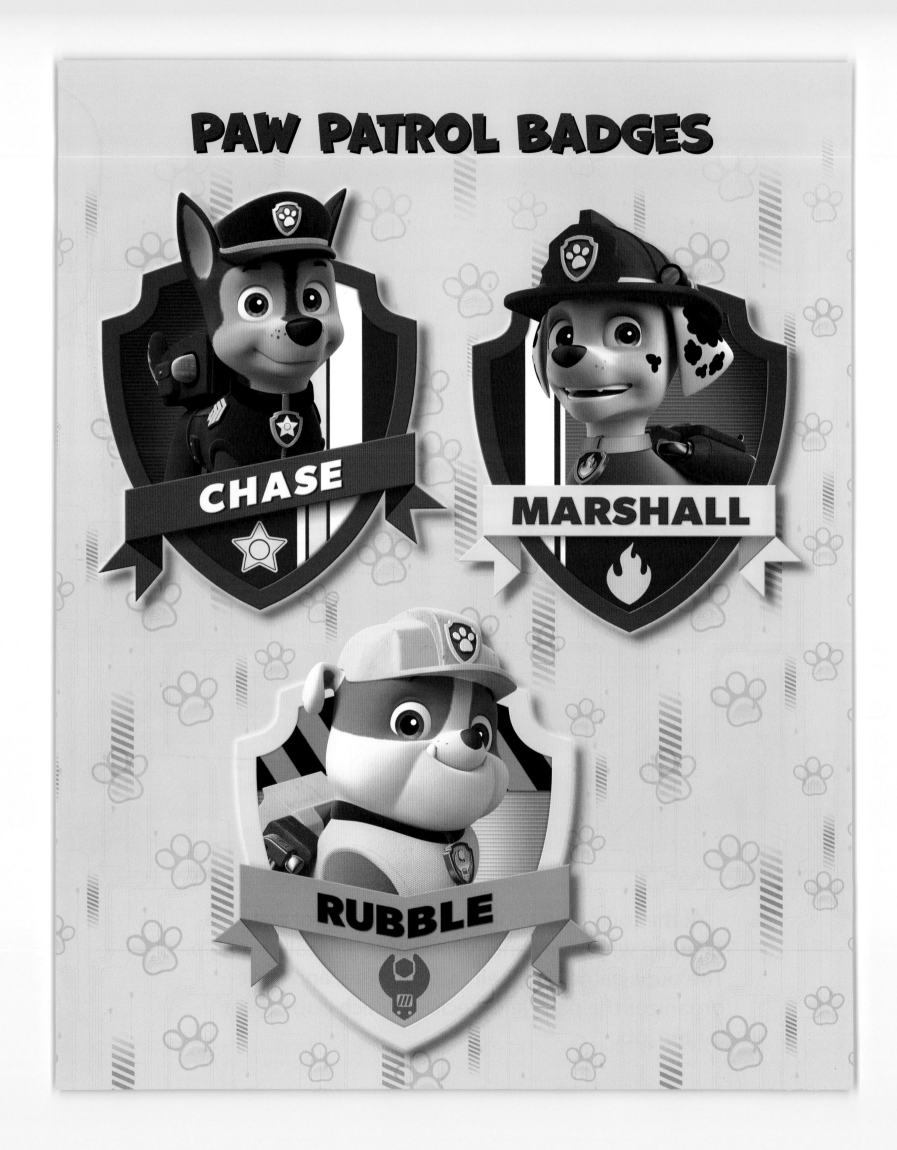

Each member of the PAW Patrol has a special badge showing what they do and how they protect the citizens of Adventure Bay.

SKYE

ROCKY

ZUMA

Whenever there's an emergency, the PAW Patrol pups line up for duty. The members of this smart, disciplined team rely on their own unique skills—and each other—to get the job done right.

After they've completed a mission, Ryder and
the pups enjoy playing in the Pup Park at the base
of the Lookout. No matter how big the adventure,
the PAW Patrol always has time for a game,
a laugh, and an ear scratch from Ryder.

The citizens of Adventure Bay are in good paws
with the PAW Patrol!